TOP SECRET

Written and illustrated by
Mick Manning and Brita Granström

Collins

During World War II many secret agents working for Britain were dropped into France. One of them was a Polish woman called Christine Granville.

The secret agents had lots of useful supplies.

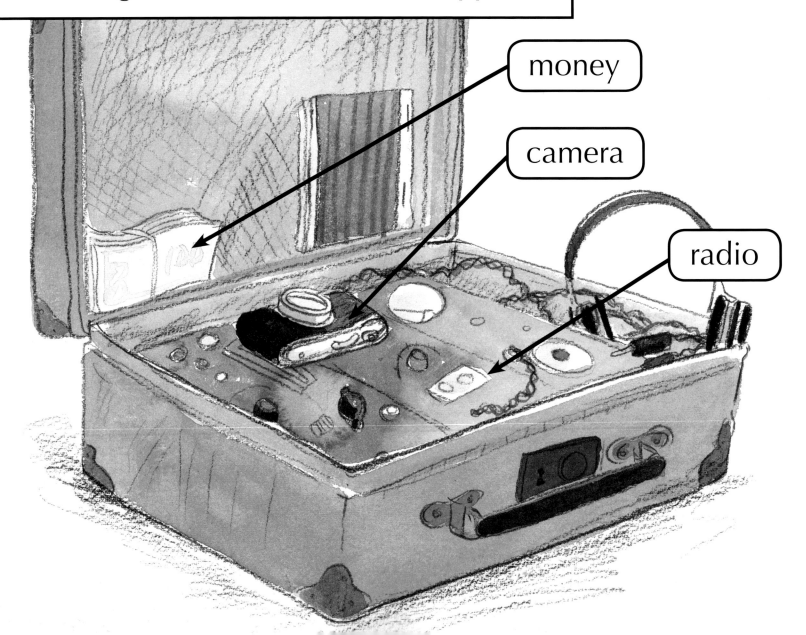

money

camera

radio

The secret agents tried lots of things to help fight the Nazis ...

collecting top secret information

sending secret messages

blowing up trains

5

blowing up bridges

Sometimes they even put itching powder in the enemy's washing.

They'll scratch for days!

7

One night the Nazis tried to capture some secret agents and one of them was Christine.

But their dog was
friendly to Christine.

9

10

Our friends have been arrested!

11

The greedy officer took the money and drove them to safety.

Christine Granville was awarded the George Cross for her bravery.

Life of a secret agent

15

Ideas for reading

Written by Gillian Howell
Primary Literacy Consultant

Learning objectives: *(reading objectives correspond with Yellow band; all other objectives correspond with Sapphire band)* use knowledge of words and spelling patterns to read unknown words; explore how writers use language for comic and dramatic effects; explore the usefulness of techniques such as visualisation in exploring the meaning of texts; reflect on how working in role helps to explore complex issues

Curriculum links: History: What can we learn about recent history by studying the life of a famous person?

High frequency words: many, for, were, one, of, them, was, a, called, jump, good, the, had, help, up, they, put, in, days, night, some, dog, but, their, to, boy, our, have, been, got, all, this, for, could, you, as, took, her

Interest words: secret agents, Britain, France, supplies, Nazis, itching powder, capture, arrested, freedom, officer, George Cross

Resources: paper, pens, paint, internet

Word count: 151

Getting started

- Read the title together and look at the cover illustration. Tell them to look at the way the woman is dressed and say what they think she is doing. Invite them to suggest when the events in this book happened and what sort of information they will find out.

- Ask them to turn to the back cover and read the blurb together. Ask the children if they think this is a true story. Spend a few moments discussing what the children already know about World War II and what secret agents did.

- Explain that this is a graphic novel with a large part of the detail contained within the illustrations. Turn to p2 and point out the speech bubble. Check that the children understand that this indicates spoken words and ask them who they think is speaking here. Ask the children to say how the words in the speech bubbles should be spoken.

Reading and responding

- Ask the children to read the book aloud but in a quiet voice. Listen in to the children as they read and prompt as necessary. Remind the children to use their knowledge of sounds to work out new or difficult vocabulary.

- When the children meet a word they struggle with, prompt them to break the word into sounds or syllables to work it out, e.g. supplies (p4), itching (p6) or capture (p8).

- Pause occasionally and ask the children to describe what is happening in the illustrations and say who they think is speaking the dialogue in the speech bubbles.